The Kingdom of Honey

Kathey Morris Mercer

PAGE PUBLISHING, INC.
New York, NY

First originally published by Page Publishing, Inc. 2019

ISBN 978-1-64584-906-3 (Paperback)
ISBN 978-1-64584-907-0 (Digital)

Printed in the United States of America

Dedication

To my loving husband, Michael, who has been my best friend for forty years and who encourages, inspires, and prays for me. You have always loved me unconditionally. I thank God for creating you just for me.

To my children, Dione Bedell and Dr. Wanita Mercer, my son-in-law, Corey; and my grandbaby, Khori Mikai; for inspiring me and insisting I write a children's book, something I am so passionate about. You guys are the best.

To my deceased mom, Juanita Morris, for showing me by example what it takes to be an amazing evangelist and prayer warrior and for always encouraging me and being my greatest fan.

To Marie Maxie, my baby sister, a triple-negative breast cancer survivor and a powerful woman of God, for showing me that prayer, faith, hope, and endurance can get you through any trial and tribulation you have in life if only you believe in God.

Once upon a time in a far, far land, there was an amazing place called the Village of Honey. This village was a part of the magical and majestic kingdom of Euphoria, and right in the middle of Euphoria was Honeyopolis, a town occupied by bees.

HONEYOPOLIS

Throughout the entire kingdom flowed a river of golden and delicious honey. The bees and the village people all took care of it, and while they worked, they worshipped God. Because of their acts of worship, love, and special care of the honey, they were very prosperous and supernaturally blessed.

For decades, the honeybees and the king had a wonderful relationship, but now violence from the outside had caused concern. The other kingdoms were fighting for more honey, and it was only a matter of time before they tried to take over the most adored kingdom in all the land. Several times they managed to slip inside the gates and destroy hundreds of bees. That was unacceptable, and the king vowed to put a stop to it.

Daily, the queen, drones, and worker bees eagerly manufactured food for the village. They enjoyed keeping the people healthy and happy, but their work had become difficult because they feared for their lives.

They believed armies from the other kingdoms were going to kill more of them. They were also concerned about storms wiping out a lot of their colonies. However, no matter what, they trusted the king to protect them, and they would not lose faith in God. They were resilient and always bounced back quickly from adversity.

The king had the power to read minds and turn the honey into gold. The streets were gold, the gates were gold, and he had the most extravagant castle in all the land—yes, made of gold.

6

The queen had an angelic voice, and weekly, the bees joined the village people at the castle to hear her sing. They loved gathering there to worship God, give thanks, and pray for their prosperity and happiness. She had the power to sing down rain so the flowers, plants, and trees would grow beautifully and the bees could pollinate.

News was spreading all over the village that the king and queen were going to have a daughter named Khori Mikai. It was proclaimed by one of the village prophets that she would have even greater powers than her parents.

When they heard Princess Khori Mikai would be born with powers as well, it was the greatest news of all and the answer to their prayers. Her name alone sent them chanting all over the village, "Princess Khori Mikai is coming! Princess Khori Mikai is coming!"

9

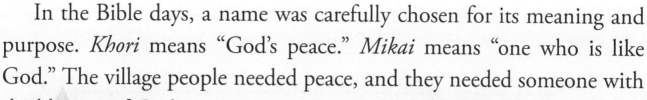

In the Bible days, a name was carefully chosen for its meaning and purpose. *Khori* means "God's peace." *Mikai* means "one who is like God." The village people needed peace, and they needed someone with the likeness of God.

They were tired of living in fear, and they desperately wanted their peace restored. So did the honeybees. They were happy to hear the princess was coming as well. They, too, believed she would save them and keep their honey supply safe.

When the princess arrived, the people cried with joy and chanted, "To God be the glory." For days and weeks, they longed to see her.

When they were finally invited to meet the princess, the soldiers escorted them to the royal throne, where the queen held her. When they looked into the princess's eyes, they were instantly filled with peace in their hearts. The fear of being harmed was gone.

Just as it had been prophesied, she was born with powers. One of her powers was giving the gift of peace. People were amazed, and they talked about it all over the village. The king understood their excitement, but he ordered them not to tell anyone outside the kingdom.

And so, as he wished, they took an oath to keep the secret and to help protect her from harm until the other powers had been revealed.

WORD SEARCH

```
H D S Y C D E S T R O Y Y K C
K E U N L E B R O L F Z T R Z
K P P D D E G X K P M V I T S
T P E S Z E T N O O F Z S E U
J I R E L Y I A I P D P R H O
P H N I A A T P R Z W Z E P R
C S A N P A C L U E A F V O E
I R T O O R N I U C P M D R P
T O U L L Q O G G C C S A P S
S W R O L L G T E A I O E A O
E E A C I T D O E L M F I D R
J J L O N M M O E C I D F H P
A U L R A K R X C S T C P I Q
M Q Y Q T E C N E L O I V C D
F W T N E I L I S E R G L P F
```

ADVERSITY

AMAZING

ANGELIC

COLONIES

DESPERATELY

DESTROY

DIFFICULTY

MAGICAL

MAJESTIC

OCCUPIED

POLLINATE

PROPHET

PROSPEROUS   PROTECT   RESILIENT

SUPERNATURALLY   VIOLENCE   WORSHIPPED

Dear parents,

Included are questions for further discussions and research:

– What was the conflict in the story?

– What sat in the middle of Euphoria?

– What power did the queen have?

– What powers did the king have?

– What did the princess's name mean?

– What power did the princess have?

– How are honeybees important to people?

– Are they becoming extinct?

– What happens if honeybees become extinct?

– What can we do to help?

Honeybees

Honeybees, what's wrong?
What could it be?
Too many of you are dying;
It's plain to see.
We can't afford to lose you.
You feed us oh so well.
For goodness sake,
We need you to pollinate.
Will someone help them?
Will someone show you care?
Something is happening.
Let's make the world aware.

Honeybees, what's wrong?
What could it be?
Are you becoming extinct?
Let's join together and demand a decree.
We can't afford to lose you.
You feed us oh so well.
For goodness sake,
We need you to pollinate.
Will someone help them?
Will someone show you care?
Something is happening.
Let's make the world aware.

Acknowledgments

Photographer—Don Hopkins
Illustrations—Lamond Hardy
Editor—Michael Mercer

About the Author

Kathey Morris Mercer is a retired educator who is passionate about teaching children to read. She is a recipient of five outstanding teacher awards in Tennessee, Alabama, and Texas and an achievement award in poetry by the International Society of Poets. She is an evangelist, private reading specialist, counselor, and motivational speaker for churches, conferences, colleges, and schools. In her spare time, she loves to write, direct, and produce musical productions as a fund-raiser for charities. She and her husband, Michael, have two daughters, a son-in-law, a granddaughter, and three four-legged grandsons. They live in San Antonio, Texas.

"Princess"

Khori Mikai

CPSIA information can be obtained
at www.ICGtesting.com
Printed in the USA
LVHW072357100720
660358LV00007B/337